Anna & Natalie

By Barbara H. Cole

Illustrated by Ronald Himler

Star Bright Books

New York

Published in the United States of America by Star Bright Books, Inc., New York.
The name Star Bright Books and the Star Bright Books logo are registered
trademarks of Star Bright Books, Inc. Please visit www.starbrightbooks.com.

ISBN-13: 978-1-59572-105-1

Printed in China (MC) 9 8 7 6 5 4 3 2 1

Library of Congress Cataloging-in-Publication Data

Cole, Barbara H.
  Anna & Natalie / by Barbara H. Cole ; illustrated by Ronald Himler.
      p. cm.
  Summary: Anna and her seeing-eye dog Natalie are chosen by Anna's teacher to participate in
the wreath-laying ceremony at the Tomb of the Unknown Soldier at Arlington National Cemetery.
  ISBN-13: 978-1-59572-105-1
  ISBN-10: 1-59572-105-3
  [1. Service dogs--Fiction. 2. War--Fiction. 3. Blind--Fiction. 4. Letters--Fiction.
5. Schools--Fiction.] I. Himler, Ronald, ill. II. Title. III. Title: Anna and Natalie.

PZ7.C673413An 2007
[Fic]--dc22
                                                                    2006036456

To all of my students, past and present,
at Sandhills Community College in Pinehurst, N.C.,
and especially to Anna and Natalie. —B.H.C.

Every year Mrs. Randall's third grade class at Willow Run School went to the Wreath-Laying Ceremony at the Tomb of the Unknown Soldier in Arlington, Virginia.

Mrs. Randall had eagle eyes to see a child's every move. She had big ears to hear those who planned mischief. She had long arms to snatch run-aheads back into line. And she had a loud voice to strike terror into the bravest daredevil.

But there was one problem. Only four students were allowed to carry the wreath in the ceremony. Which four would they be?

Four students would walk down the long white marble steps to the tomb with a huge crowd of people watching. To be selected meant feeling like the most special person in the whole world.

Mrs. Randall said, "If you really want to be on the Tomb Team," which is what she called it, "then write me a letter and tell me why you should be selected. It's due first thing in the morning."

"I don't like writing letters. I'm out," called out Freddie.

"Me neither," added Tommy.

"I like writing letters," chimed in Nancy. "And mine will be the best."

Anna was quiet. She always wanted to be chosen for the teams at school, but mostly never was. She was never picked for the softball team. Never asked to be on the basketball team. Never a cheerleader. Never in the class play. Never chosen to play Red Rover, Red Rover, Come-Over.

Sure, someone always chose her for the spelling team. But the others—the fun ones—never. Never. Never.

And Anna knew better than to ask.

But this time something deep inside told her to try. Maybe she would be picked this time.

All day Anna dreamed through the lessons, and Mrs. Randall's eagle eyes saw it.

"Anna, get your mind back on your work. You seem a thousand miles away."

"Yes, Ma'am. I am. I'm sorry." But in no time at all, she was dreaming and planning again. Mrs. Randall had said to write a letter, and she'd write that letter all right.

It seemed like ten years until the bell rang to go home.

When the school bus dropped Anna and her sister off, they hurried home, faster than ever before.

"Natalie," Anna said, "We're going to be on that Tomb Team. I promise. I've got a plan, but we've got a lot of work to do."

"How are my favorite girls?" Mom asked when they got home. "How was school today?"

"Wonderful," Anna beamed. Natalie just sat down and groaned.

Mom said, "Tell me about it."

"There's a contest," Anna said excitedly, "and I think we can win. Anyway, I'm going to try, starting right now. But first I need to call Grandpa for some help that no one else can give me."

"What kind of help?" Mom asked.

"It's a secret," Anna said.

Then she called Grandpa and went to her bedroom to talk. When Anna got off the phone, she said, "Come on, Nat, let's go sit on the porch."

Anna settled into the big rocker, and Natalie, as usual, lay on the swing. "You're so lazy," Anna said, "but it's okay. We will win. Just you wait and see."

Natalie drew a long breath, settled down, and closed her eyes.

Anna rocked a while, thinking. Then she took her computer out of her book bag and started her letter.

"Dear Mrs. Randall..."

The words came easily.

Anna wrote and Natalie slept. The shadows were long, and the day was almost over when Anna said, "Okay, Nat, that's all. You can wake up now, you lazy thing. We're going to win! Just you wait and see."

Natalie stretched and yawned, her big brown eyes turning to Anna.

Anna folded the letter and put it in the long white envelope her mother had given her. She wrote *"Mrs. Randall"* across the front.

First thing the next day, Mrs. Randall took the letters. Everyone except Tommy and Freddie had written one.

"I will tell you who the four winners are tomorrow," Mrs. Randall said. "This will be a hard decision to make because I know you all want to win."

The class shouted, "Yes! Yes!"

"Remember," Mrs. Randall said, "it certainly is an honor to be on the team, but it is also an honor to visit the Tomb."

Sometimes Mrs. Randall let the lessons wait while she told them other important things. Today was one of those wonderful days. They talked about Washington and the monuments and the Capitol and the White House, but especially they talked about the Tomb of the Unknown Soldier and the Changing of the Guard.

The next day at school, Mrs. Randall finally said, "I'm ready to announce the Tomb Team winners. It was a difficult decision, and you must remember this team will represent us all. They will march, and we will stand at attention. We're really all one big team. There were four excellent letters, but I will read just one to you."

"Dear Mrs. Randall,
    I want to be on the team, not for myself, but for many others who have not been honored or remembered. They worked long and hard and saved many lives. Sometimes they were wounded and had to be sewed up and sent home."

Mrs. Randall did not correct the mistake. She just read on as if it was correct to say *sewed up*.

"And sometimes they were heroes bigger than the strongest men around. Sometimes they carried medicine and food to dangerous places to save the wounded soldiers. My own great-great-grandfather was in this special service and saved lives. I would like to be on the team to say thank you to those forgotten heroes of World War II.
        Yours truly..."

Mrs. Randall's voice cracked and choked, and then she read,
        "From Natalie (with help from Anna)"

The class clapped their hands and shouted, "Yeah, Natalie! Yeah, Natalie!"

"But wait, class, there's another sentence in this letter."

"P.S.—Would you please let Anna walk with me so I will not be alone and she won't be either?"

The class shouted, "Yeah, Anna! Yeah, Anna!" All of a sudden, Anna felt like a jumping bean. This meant she and Natalie would be on the team just as she had dreamed.

Anna's family was as proud as could be, and Grandpa said, "We'll all go to the Wreath-Laying Ceremony. With two of our girls in it, we all need to be there. We can take pictures."

At last, the day came when Mrs. Randall and the class climbed the
long hill at Arlington Cemetery to lay their wreath at the Tomb of the
Unknown Soldier. The girls wore their prettiest dresses and the boys
wore shirts and ties and Sunday slacks. Natalie led the procession down
the long marble steps, her black coat glistening and her brass buttons
shining like the sun. Anna walked beside her.

At the bottom of the steps, a soldier handed the Tomb Team the beautiful wreath of dogwood flowers, magnolias, and decorative red birds that Mrs. Randall had brought with them. In a loud voice, he said, "The students of Willow Run School and Natalie, a seeing-eye dog, will lay this wreath to honor the men who served in World War II and the dogs who helped them. *ATTENTION!*"

The children put their hands over their hearts and the bugler played *Taps*.

When the last note sounded, Grandpa took a picture of the Tomb Team. He also took one of Anna and Natalie as they stood before the Tomb of the Unknown Soldier.

The whole family would always remember this shining moment of Anna, and of Natalie, who saw the world that Anna could not see.

DOGS IN WAR

The remarkable qualities of a dog—its keen senses, watchfulness, speed, compliant attitude, loyalty and affection for man—enable it to be a useful companion in war. The early Greek and Roman soldiers used attack dogs, frequently equipped with armor or spiked collars. Napoleon used dogs as sentries at the gates of Alexandria. By the early twentieth century, most European countries were using dogs in their armies. During World War I, both sides of the conflict used dogs.

The first recorded American Canine Corp was started in 1835. During the Civil War, dogs were used as messengers, guards, and mascots. But not until World War II were dogs used to help the fighting men. The dogs were trained for sentry, messenger, scout, sled and pack duties.

In 1942, the U.S. opened the "K-9 Corps," the first military dog training center. In the war zone, the dogs, usually German Shepherds and Dobermans, served as guard dogs, scouting ahead of troops, delivering messages and medicine, alerting soldiers to danger, and even attacking enemy soldiers. Scout and messenger dogs were used in reconnaissance work and warned soldiers of the presence of the enemy. Dogs were used to detect mines, trip wires, and booby traps, and thus helped save many lives. Dogs who patrolled with soldiers helped to protect them from ambush and boosted their morale. During World War II, more than 10,000 American dogs and thousands of Red Cross dogs from many other countries were used.

Approximately 4,000 dogs were used in the Vietnam War. They served as scouts, sentries, mine and tunnel detectors, and in search-and-rescue missions. It is believed that during the Vietnam War as many as 10,000 men were saved by dogs. And in Iraq, War Dogs are serving with the men and women in the army.

Although there are a number of small memorials, the National War Dog Memorial Fund, launched in April 2001, aims to build a national memorial in Washington, D.C. to honor the service of America's brave dogs.